*This book
belongs to*

_____

_____

# The
# First Little
# Fairy

## AND OTHER FAIRY STORIES

# The First Little Fairy

## AND OTHER FAIRY STORIES

First published in Great Britain in 1998 by
Parragon
13 Whiteladies Road
Clifton
Bristol BS8 1PB

ISBN 0 75252-530-1

Printed in Great Britain

Produced by Nicola Baxter
PO Box 71
Diss Norfolk IP22 2DT

Stories by Nicola Baxter
Designed by Amanda Hawkes
Text illustrations by Duncan Gutteridge
Cover illustration by Alisa Tingley

# Contents

# The
# First Little
# Fairy

There was a time, long ago, when there were no fairies in the world. Mother Nature had no little helpers and had to do all her work by herself. As you know, fairies now help that grand old lady in many, many ways. They sprinkle dew drops on the grass in the early morning. They sweep the autumn leaves into piles that we can rustle with our feet. They mend broken spiders' webs and coax shy little flowers to open every morning.

In fact, all fairies are specially fond of flowers, and that is because the very first fairy in the world was born from a little woodland flower herself. Ever since then, fairies have almost always been given flower names.

When the world was young, Mother Nature made sure that all living things knew the part they had to play on our wonderful earth. Flowers understood that they must grow and send out buds to open beautifully in the

sunshine. Trees knew that they must grow straight and tall, stretching their branches out to shelter the little creatures living beneath them. Mother Nature taught the first birds to fly, so that they in turn could teach their own children. She showed them where to build their nests and how to hatch their eggs. She showed rabbits how to dig burrows and caterpillars how to turn into butterflies. There was no part of nature, from the tiniest ant to the largest elephant that was not guided and helped by her loving hands. And everything flourished.

When living things were in harmony, all was well, but soon life on earth began to change. Human beings ploughed up the earth and planted crops. They rooted out lovely wildflowers, calling them weeds. Instead they grew food for themselves and their animals, not thinking about the rest of nature at all.

Later on, humans built villages and towns. The smoke from their fires drifted up and sometimes hid the sun itself, which helps Mother Nature to give life to all the plants and animals on our planet. Buildings crushed the land beneath them, driving out the creatures that had lived where now streets and houses covered the earth.

As time went on, humans began to throw rubbish into the rivers, making it hard for fish to live. They chopped down trees and rooted up grasslands. Everywhere they went, they seemed to want to change Mother Nature's careful work. The poor old lady wept to see what had become of her beautiful world.

One day, Mother Nature sat in a woodland glade and buried her head in her hands in despair. There was just too much for her to do. She could not put all the ills of the world right by herself. While she was rescuing the fish from a dirty river, little animals were losing their homes as trees were destroyed. Mother Nature knew that she could not hold back the damage caused by man for ever. She felt powerless and very much alone.

On the other side of the glade, a little flower was growing. She remembered how Mother Nature had saved her only the year before. Winds had caused a huge bough to fall from the mighty tree above, crushing her beneath its weight. Mother Nature had gently lifted the branch and freed the bruised leaves of the plant. She had sprinkled her buds with sunlight and moonshine, until a few weeks later, the plant had flowered in the most beautiful way. The flower could not forget Mother Nature's kindness.

Now the old lady sat miserably in the woodland. The little flower could not bear to see her friend so very upset.

"If only I could do something to help her," said the flower to herself. "But I am only a little flower. I cannot move from this spot even to comfort Mother Nature. What a poor thing I am!"

Now it so happened that just at that moment, a tiny amount of stardust fell to earth. And when stardust falls on any living thing that is making a wish, the wish always comes true. As the little flower wished she could be free to help her friend, the stardust shimmered over her leaves and petals. Almost at once, the flower felt something wonderful happen.

One of her blooms began to take on a life of its own. Its yellow petals became a little dress, as delicate as gossamer. Its fragile green leaves became a tiny cloak, as light as a feather. From the centre of the flower, a beautiful little face peeped out. And most wonderful of all, the stardust itself formed two glittering wings that shimmered in the sunlight.

Without a sound, the first little fairy fluttered up into the air, flew swiftly across the clearing, and settled on Mother Nature's shoulder. She lay her little face against the old lady's worn cheek to comfort her and let her know

that help was at hand. Mother
Nature was no longer alone.

"I will help you all I can," said
the first little fairy. Her voice was
so gentle and small that the old
lady could hardly hear it.

Mother Nature looked up and
thought that she had seen many
lovely things, but this little
creature was fairer than any of
them. That is why she decided to
call her tiny helper a *fairy*.

"I am sure that other flowers
will do what they can to help
you, when they see me," said the
little fairy kindly. And she was
right. Soon bluebells, foxgloves,
cowslips, poppies and all the

other lovely flowers of the world
were growing little fairies of their
own, each prettier and more
graceful than the last. They
fluttered around Mother Nature,
waiting for her to tell them what
to do to help to make the world
a more beautiful place.

And the wise old lady taught
each fairy to help in the places
she knew best, so that woodland
bluebells became Bluebell
Fairies, flying up to take food to
mother birds who could not
leave the eggs they were keeping
warm. Poppy Fairies flutter into
cornfields to warn the little mice
who live there that the farmer is

coming to cut the corn. You may have seen their little red dresses flitting through a field of golden yellow grain in summer.

As for the first little fairy, she always stays by Mother Nature's side, helping her to talk to the fairies she meets – for sometimes their voices are so tiny that the old lady cannot hear them at all – and explaining to new fairies how the wide and wonderful world of nature works.

So, if you *almost* think you see a flicker of green and yellow among the leaves, remember Mother Nature and the very first fairy.

# The
# Fairy Who
# Couldn't
# Fly

Once upon a time, there was a Foxglove Fairy who had a darling little daughter. All babies are sweet, as they lie so trustingly in their mothers' arms, but fairy babies are even more lovable. They are very tiny, for one thing. You can put them to bed in half a walnut shell and still have plenty of room for a tiny teddy bear and a seedhead rattle.

The Foxglove Fairy called her baby daughter Little Foxglove, which is what fairies tend to do. Sometimes it is very confusing, because you may have, say, Tiny Foxglove, Little Foxglove, Medium-Sized Foxglove, Big

Foxglove and just plain Foxglove all in one family. But fairies know who is who, and that is the most important thing.

Anyway, the Little Foxglove in this story was a very contented child. She lay in her cradle and chuckled and waved her little fists. I don't know if you have ever been out in the countryside at night, but if you have, you'll know that the air is full of strange little cries. People will tell you that they are mice, and owls, and other little creatures, going about their business, but between you are me, at least some of those sounds are baby fairies! Little Foxglove, however, hardly ever cried.

"She is *such* a good baby," Foxglove told her friend Cowslip. "She is so happy all the time. Look at her now, gurgling and cooing in her cradle."

Foxglove had covered her baby's little bed in the finest gossamer and trimmed it with ribbons made of rose petals.

"She certainly is a good baby," said Cowslip, whose own child was rather a handful, "but I don't suppose it will last. All children are trouble at one time or another." (Ask your mother or father about this. Is it true?)

But Little Foxglove was soon sitting up and playing with her toys. She would wave her little fists at visitors and say "Bye Bye", which could sometimes be a little bit embarrassing if it wasn't time for them to go yet!

Still Little Foxglove was the happiest, cuddliest baby for

miles around, and Foxglove was hugely proud of her.

But one day, when she went to visit her friend Cowslip, Foxglove walked into the parlour and felt something small and soft bump into her tummy. It was Little Cowslip, and she was flying! Of course, because she had only just started, she wasn't very good at it yet, which is why she had bumped into Foxglove, but still, her little wings were carrying her up into the air, and she was getting better at fluttering and floating and flying round corners every day. She looked *so* grown up!

"How is Little Foxglove's flying coming along?" asked Cowslip, as she sat down with her friend for a cup of cornflower tea.

"Well," said Foxglove, feeling that she must tell the truth, "she hasn't really started yet. All babies learn things at different times. I expect she will make her first little flutters any day now."

But the days passed, and Little Foxglove didn't show any signs of wanting to fly. She toddled around on her fat little legs and enjoyed helping her mummy with all kinds of things, but she didn't seem interested in flapping her dear little wings.

Foxglove tried all kinds of things to tempt her daughter into the air. She carried her in her arms as she herself flew around the house and outside. She showed Little Foxglove all the interesting things there were to be seen above the ground. But the baby, although she enjoyed her little flights, didn't want to try to fly herself.

Then Foxglove tried hanging all kinds of tempting little treats from the ceiling of her home, hoping that Little Foxglove would want to fly up and grab them in her podgy little fingers. But after a visiting fairy bumped her nose on a hanging apple ring, Foxglove had to take them down again. In any case, Little Foxglove hadn't been in the least bit interested in them.

"Still not flying?" asked Cowslip, when she visited again. "Have you seen the goblin doctor?"

"Yes," replied Foxglove, wishing that her friend had not raised the subject. "He says that Little Foxglove is fine and will fly in her own good time."

Cowslip looked at the little fairy, who was watching Little Cowslip as she flitted expertly around the room. "She is rather plump," she said. "No doubt there is a lot of weight for her little wings to lift."

"Little Foxglove is cuddly, not plump," said the proud mother sharply. "She will fly in her own good time. All the fairies in my family were late flyers."

"Really?" said Cowslip. "It is quite the opposite with *us*."

Little Foxglove waved her chubby hands at Cowslip and said, "Bye Bye!" And for once her mother agreed with her!

The weeks passed, and winter turned into spring. Everywhere you looked, little creatures were building nests or making cosy homes in holes and hollows.

They were all settling down to
have their babies.

Foxglove loved this time of
year. She showed her little
daughter a robin's nest, cleverly
built in the top of an old kettle
that a human had left lying
about. She carried the little fairy

quietly up into the branches of an apple tree to see a blackbird's nest. And she let Little Foxglove peep down a burrow under a hawthorn hedge, where a proud mummy rabbit already had eight little babies!

Little Foxglove loved to see all these little creatures. Foxglove was pleased to see how gentle her little girl was with all the living things she met.

"You are a real little fairy," she whispered, hugging her tight, "in all the ways that matter. There is plenty of time for you to learn to fly. Don't you worry. We won't listen to Cowslip."

And Little Foxglove would look up and laugh in the jolliest way imaginable, as if to say, "I'm not worried about learning to fly. It doesn't bother *me*!"

The spring days grew warmer. Soon it was that wonderful time of the year when it is not quite spring and not quite summer. The air is warm on your face, but everything is still fresh and green and new.

Foxglove took her little fairy to play in a woodland glade while she busied herself collecting eggshells. When the baby birds in their nests above hatched out, their mothers threw the empty eggshells down on to the ground below. You may find some yourself one year, but only if you are quick and look before the fairies have come around gathering, for fairies like to collect the little eggshells to make into useful things at home. They often drink their tea out of eggshell cups and eat their honeydew out of eggshell basins.

As Little Foxglove played in the mossy glade, her mother flitted here and there, putting the pretty pieces of blue, green and white eggshell that she found into a large basket. She kept Little Foxglove in sight all the time.

After a while, Little Foxglove became more interested in what was happening above her in the trees than she was in her toys on the ground. For high up on the branch of a birch tree, a real commotion was going on.

Most birds had already hatched and raised one little family. Now their babies had flown away to make homes of their own, so some birds were having another family while the evenings were still light and the sun was still warm.

High above the clearing, a mother bird had flown off to find food for her three hungry nestlings, and while she was gone, one of them, bolder than the rest, decided that he would like to try to fly. He really was being a silly little bird, for his feathers had not yet grown properly, and his little wings were not very strong. Still, some little birds don't have the sense they were hatched with, and this one was quite determined that he would hop over the edge of the nest and flutter down to the ground beneath. It didn't look very far, and he thought how proud his mother would be when she returned. Of course, if his mother had been present, she would have put a stop to such experiments in no uncertain terms. Baby birds, like baby fairies, must fly when they arc ready, and not a moment sooner.

As Little Foxglove looked up, the baby bird flapped his little wings and *jumped*.

It was clear a split second later that he had made a dreadful mistake. His little wings flapped uselessly, and he began to fall, down, down, towards the hard tree roots below.

But in the twinkling of an eye, there was a shimmer and a flutter, and Little Foxglove flew up and caught the little bird in her arms. Then she flew on up to the nest on the branch and gently popped the silly bird back into his cosy home with his brother and sister. Little Foxglove fluttered back down towards the ground, but because she felt happy that she had been able to help, she did a victory circuit of the whole clearing. You have never seen such beautiful flying in your life.

Standing below, Foxglove felt her eyes fill with tears as her little girl came gently to rest. Now she wasn't a baby any more, but a real little girl, and a very fine fairy indeed.

# Fairy
# Footprints

There was once a little girl who was very interested in fairies. More than anything else, she longed to meet a real live fairy herself. The little girl was called Emily, and she spent a lot of time looking out for clues that a fairy was nearby.

One day, Emily's mother saw her crawling along the ground with a magnifying glass in her hand, peering at the carpet.

"What *are* you doing, Emily? she asked.

"I'm looking for fairy footprints," explained the little girl. "They're very tiny, so I need a magnifying glass to see them."

"But do fairies leave footprints?" asked Emily's father, who had come in just as Emily was explaining.

"Of course they do," said Emily. *"We* leave footprints. So why shouldn't fairies?"

"Well, what if they're flying?" asked her father. "There wouldn't be any footprints then."

Emily was very quiet for a moment. She hadn't thought of that, and, of course, Daddy was perfectly right. It would be much more sensible for a fairy to fly wherever she had to go. Emily's face fell. She was never going to find a fairy footprint.

Emily's mother and father saw her disappointed little face and felt sorry for her. They wished they had let her carry on with her game without interruptions.

That night, when Mummy tucked Emily into bed, she picked up her favourite fairy story book as usual to read to her. But Emily pushed it away.

"I don't want to read about fairies any more," she said. "I'm never going to see one, so what's the point?"

Mummy tried to persuade the little girl to read her book as usual, but Emily had made up her mind. She turned over and

shut her eyes, looking most
unhappy. She didn't even say
goodnight to Mummy.

Emily's mother crept away, feeling rather upset. She felt that it was somehow her fault that her little girl was so miserable. Back in the dining room, she told her husband what had happened.

"Poor little girl," he said. "We should have left her with her dreams. Isn't there anything we can do to make her feel better?"

"Apart from finding some fairy footprints, I don't think there is," said his wife.

Emily's mother and father looked at each. Then they both grinned at the same time.

"How are we going to do it?" asked her father.

They had decided to make some pretend fairy footprints for Emily to find. Even if they weren't *real* footprints, they would make Emily happy again, and that was the most important thing. But how could they do it?

Then Mummy remembered that Emily had a tiny fairy doll with little fairy shoes.

"If we pressed one of those on an ink pad from Emily's printing kit, we could make footprints all along the windowsill," she said.

After waiting half an hour to be sure that Emily was asleep, her mummy crept into the little girl's bedroom and borrowed the fairy

doll from Emily's toy cupboard.
It was harder to find the ink pad
from the printing kit in the dark,
but she found it at last (and left
inky fingerprints over the inside
of the cupboard door).

Back in the dining room, Emily's
mother and father practised on a
piece of paper. Soon they were
quite good at making fairy
footprints. It was time to put
their skills to good use.

This time both parents crept
into the little girl's room. They
carefully opened the curtains of
her window. Luckily, it was a
moonlit night. The moonlight
shone on to the windowsill,

showing it as clearly as could be.
Very, very carefully, Daddy made
the first few footsteps.

"Watch out!" whispered
Mummy. "We mustn't leave any
smudges. That would give the
game away!"

At last there was a neat set of
footprints on the windowsill. It
looked as though a little fairy
had peeped through the curtains

at Emily, to see that she was all
right. The footprints led right to
the edge of the windowsill, then
stopped completely.

Mummy and Daddy crept
away, leaving Emily to sleep.
They couldn't wait to see what
happened in the morning.

Now there is a very strange
thing about this story. And that
is that Mummy and Daddy made
the footprints because they
really did not believe in fairies.
They did not believe that Emily
would *ever* meet a real fairy, but
they wanted to make her happy
by pretending that there had
been one in her room.

And the even stranger thing is that there *was* a fairy in Emily's bedroom! Yes, a little fairy called Marigold lived on top of Emily's wardrobe. Her job in the little girl's home was to look after the houseplants that Mummy forgot to water and to make sure that Emily's puppy and rabbit were properly looked after.

Marigold watched as Emily's mother and father made the fairy footprints. She couldn't understand *what* they were doing. When they had left the room, she flew down from her perch and peered at the painted windowsill. How very odd! The two grown-ups had been making tiny footprints! Suddenly, the little fairy understood what they had been doing, and she was very, very angry.

Marigold took the cloth that Emily used to clean her chalkboard and wiped the fairy footprints away. How dare those grown-ups pretend that a fairy with huge feet had walked across the windowsill? Fairies pride themselves on never leaving a mess behind – not so much as a footprint, or a fingerprint, or a strand of their silky hair. Their job is to help the living things of the world, not to make messy marks themselves. Marigold sat down and wondered what to do.

First of all, she decided, she must make sure that Emily believed in fairies again. It is really important that children love fairies, for it helps the little people to do their work. Marigold crept on to Emily's bed and skipped up to where her little head lay on the pillow. Then she bent down and began to whisper in Emily's ear.

Marigold's whispering brought Emily the loveliest dream she had ever had. She dreamed she was in fairyland, talking to all her fairy friends. When she woke up in the morning, she could remember every detail of the wonderful dream.

"Now I know that there really are fairies," she said with a smile.

But a few hours before, while it was still dark, Marigold decided to teach Emily's mother and father a lesson too. She hurried into the sitting room and saw that the soot from the fire was cold but had not yet been swept up. Carefully, she dipped her dainty little feet into the soot, then she fluttered her wings and flew straight to Emily's parents' bedroom upstairs. Can you guess what that clever little fairy did

then? Quite against her training
and all the fairy lore, she ran
lightly across the white cover on
the bed, leaving little black
footprints behind her. She knew
that the cover could be washed,
and no real harm had been done,
but she wanted to teach those
cheeky grown-ups that fairy
footprints are a serious matter, not
something to be made a joke of.

When she had finished making
her footprints, Marigold flew to
the bathroom and washed her
dirty little shoes in soapy water.
They were soon as good as new,
and she hung them on the
radiator to dry, intending to pick

them up before morning. The little shoes were so tiny that they dried very quickly.

The next day dawned bright and clear. Emily's Mummy and Daddy woke up and had a little argument about whose turn it was to go and make the tea. In fact, whenever there was an argument, it was always because it was really Emily's father's turn. In the end, he hopped out of bed and put on his dressing gown.

Emily's father was just about to leave the room when he noticed what looked like some dirty marks on the bedcover. He bent forward to take a closer look and let out a small whistle of surprise.

"What is it?" asked Emily's mother, sitting up in bed.

"What do you make of this?" asked her husband.

"Has that puppy been on the bed again?" cried Emily's mother.

"No, I don't think so," her husband replied. "These marks are much too tiny, but they are definitely footprints."

Then both the grown-ups remembered the trick they had played on Emily the night before.

"She must have found the footprints and known it was us," said the little girl's father. "Then she came and made these little footprints in the same way for revenge. What a clever little girl!"

But Emily's mother was looking more closely at the marks.

"These are much smaller than the ones we made," she said, "and Emily doesn't have a doll that is smaller than her fairy doll. The only thing that could have made prints as small as these is…"

"Yes?" asked her husband.

"… is a *real* fairy!"

"Oh, that's ridiculous," cried Emily's daddy. "There are no such things as fairies. You know that, darling."

"Do I?" asked his wife. "You know, now that I've seen this, I'm not too sure."

"I'm going to settle this once and for all," said Emily's daddy, hurrying across the landing to his little girl's room. He could have sworn that everything was exactly as he and his wife had left it the night before, but the footprints on the windowsill were quite definitely gone.

"It's settled," he told his wife. "Emily woke in the night and saw the footprints on her windowsill. She realised it was us and decided to give us a taste of our own medicine. There are quite definitely no such things as fairies. Now I suggest we don't discuss it any more. Personally, I feel too silly about what we did to want to mention it to Emily."

So Emily never did know that there had been fake fairy footprints on her windowsill. She didn't know that she had a fairy living on top of her wardrobe either, although sometimes she almost thought she saw the flicker of little silver wings.

Emily's mother still wasn't sure what she thought, but her father was quite sure – until he found two tiny little slippers in the bathroom when he went to shave!

# The Tooth Fairy's Problem

Have you ever had a visit from the tooth fairy? Perhaps you have not yet lost any of your baby teeth. When you do, you should put your old tooth under your pillow or in a little bag when you go to sleep that night. The tooth fairy will come and take away your old tooth, leaving you a little surprise in return.

Now this job, as you can imagine, keeps the tooth fairy very busy. There are lots of children all over the world, and at some time or another, every one of them loses some teeth. Then the tooth fairy has to make sure she visits them all before morning. Luckily, while one part of the world is in darkness, another part is enjoying the middle of the day, so the tooth fairy only has to concentrate on half the world at a time. But that is still an awful lot of teeth for her to collect!

Now the tooth fairy is no bigger than any of the other

fairies on earth. She finds it quite easy to carry a little baby tooth from the front of your mouth. Teeth from the back of your mouth are much bigger, so sometimes the tooth fairy has rather a struggle to carry the tooth back to fairyland.

After working very hard one week last winter, the tooth fairy felt that she could not go on any more. She went to Mother Nature and explained her problem.

"I don't know what to do," she said. "Are the children of the world getting bigger? It feels to me as though their teeth are becoming heavier and heavier. I can hardly lift them to bring them back to fairyland. After working all day, I have to visit some of the children in the other half of the world, so I hardly ever get any sleep. And with all those heavy teeth, I'm becoming very tired. In fact, I'm exhausted."

"Oh dear, that will never do," said Mother Nature. "Let me think about this, my dear, and I will give you my opinion in a little while. Come back to see me at this time tomorrow, and I will see what I can do."

"Thank you, Mother Nature," replied the tooth fairy. "I shall return tomorrow. Goodbye!"

Mother Nature thought long and hard about the difficulty, but she could not imagine how to solve it. Even if she found more fairy helpers for the tooth fairy (and it is a very specialised job that not all fairies can do), she could not do anything about the heaviness of the teeth.

After thinking for a long time, Mother Nature became tired. She decided to go for a walk to clear her head. It was very pleasant in the countryside. Old Mother Nature walked along beside a stream, seeing meadows full of flowers and trees spreading out their green leaves in the

sunshine. In fact, it was so pleasant that Mother Nature decided to sit down for a rest. In no time at all, she had fallen fast asleep on a grassy bank.

Now Mother Nature works just as hard as the tooth fairy, so it was not surprising that she felt tired in the middle of the day, but her sleep did not last for long. As the old lady took in a deep breath, she felt something tickling her nose, and she woke up. *Atishooo!* Mother Nature sneezed the tickle away.

But as Mother Nature was getting to her feet, she felt another tickle on her nose. Looking up, she saw that the air was full of dandelion seeds, each floating below its own parachute of fluffy silk. It was one of these that had made Mother Nature sneeze a few moments before.

As she watched the little seeds bobbing in the air, Mother Nature had a wonderful idea.

Next day, when the tooth fairy came to call on Mother Nature, she found the old lady hard at work. She seemed to be talking very seriously to a group of Dandelion Fairies.

"Now, my dears," she said, "you understand what you have to do? It is mainly a question of co-ordination. As long as you talk to each other and to the tooth fairy, we shall never have a problem of under- or over-supply, shall we?"

"No, Mother Nature," replied the Dandelion Fairies, bobbing little curtseys in their yellow frilly dresses.

It was not long before Mother Nature had explained to the tooth fairy that the Dandelion Fairies would attach dandelion seeds to all the large teeth. This would make them float in the air, so that they would be easier for the tooth fairy to carry.

"That's a wonderful idea!" said the tooth fairy. "You are clever, Mother Nature."

"No, no," said the old lady. "Nature is clever. I just do what I can to help."

So if, in the night after you lose one of your baby teeth, you suddenly sneeze, you will know what has been happening!

# The Fairyland Fair

Sometimes the fairies all over the world seem to be in a flutter. If you half close your eyes when you are out in the countryside, you may see them flitting here and there, looking busier and more excited than usual. That's because it's time for the Fairyland Fair.

The Fairyland Fair is a wonderful event. All the fairies that can possibly manage it come along, and that is a lot of fairies. In fairy time, the Fair lasts for three days, but in human time, that is only about three minutes, so humans do not usually notice that all the fairies

have disappeared for a little
while. Since most humans never
see a fairy in all their lives, very
few people know about the
Fairyland Fair. I thought you
might like to share this fairy
secret. Be careful who else you
tell, won't you?

Now the Fairyland Fair is like
human fairs in lots of ways, but
in other ways it is very different.
There are stalls and sideshows.
Fairies love to play games like
"Knock the poppy head off the
turnip" or "Find the hidden
mustard seed". There are
fairground rides, too, with the
dearest little swinging boats

made from peanut shells and a roundabout with hanging hazlenut shells to sit in. Of course, only fairies can fit on the rides, which is one reason why only fairies are invited.

It came as a shock to the Fair Committee (chaired by Mother Nature) one year to find that several little elves had been caught disguising themselves as fairies in order to come to the Fairyland Fair. In fact, no one would have discovered this at all, if one little elf had not been found sleeping under the "Guess the weight of the acorn" stall. She had already changed back

into her elfin clothes, but her
fairy disguise was lying beside her.
Just a minute, you will say.
Elves don't look anything like
fairies! They have pointed ears
for one thing and absolutely no

wings at all. Well, that's true, but when an elf has on a sweet little fairy cap of sky-blue petals and is wearing a cloak of green velvet, it is very hard to tell that he or she is not a fairy.

You may be wondering, too, why it should matter that elves attended the Fairyland Fair. There is, I'm afraid, a history of coolness between elves and fairies. It started when elves were heard to say that fairies were *silly*. Now, like me, you have probably met a great many elves who are much, much sillier than any fairy in the world, but that is not how elves see it. Just as they have always thought that goblins are fierce and a little frightening, they have always considered fairies to be silly and not very clever. And this just goes to show how careful you must be to find out if what you hear about a person is true or just a story, for goblins are not in the least bit fierce, and fairies are some of the cleverest little people I know.

For a long time, in her early days, Mother Nature tried to be friendly with the elves. She hoped that they too might help her in her work. But elves are much more interested in their own lives and customs. They do not care for nature as fairies do. In fact, even goblins are better informed about how the world works that elves are. That is why goblins often make very good doctors, and even fairies call on them if they are ever sick or hurt. And that is about the only thing that elves and fairies have in common, for elves too use goblin doctors whenever they need them.

And what do fairies think of elves? Well, of course, no one likes to know that someone thinks they are silly and stupid. Fairies, not unnaturally, resent the unthinking views of most elves. Quite often, the elves that talk most frequently about the silliness of fairies are the very same elves that have never in their lives met one!

When she heard that elves had been visiting the Fairyland Fair, Mother Nature did not know what to do. She was a dear and friendly old lady, as you know, and she would have liked to have invented all the elves who wanted to come – and goblins too, for that matter. But Mother Nature also knew that where lots of elves are gathered together, there is often *trouble*. And the last thing that Mother Nature wanted at the wonderful Fairyland Fair was any kind of commotion or difficulty.

In view of this, a notice was put up on a tree at the outskirts of the Fair.

# Fairyland Fair

## Fairies only.

## Elves not welcome.

### By order of the Fair Committee.

Now this notice was not very friendly. It might have been better if someone had explained to the elves why they were not welcome. As it was, they took one look at the notice and declared that they wanted nothing to do with such snooty fairies. Such a notice, they said, only proved how silly fairies were, for any fair at which elves were present was bound to be superior to a fairies-only event.

Mother Nature was not very happy about the notice either, but she could not think of anything else to do. She could not bear to think of there being trouble at the Fairyland Fair.

Strangely enough, it was this very notice that ended the bad feeling between the elves and the fairies. It happened like this.

Fairies, on the whole, do what they are told by Mother Nature. They are not argumentative by nature, and they feel happiest when they are helping another living creature.

Elves, on the other hand, will argue at the drop of a hat. At the first sign of a disagreement, they will call an elfin meeting. This gathering gives everyone a chance to put forward his or her views, but the disadvantage is that the meeting can last for days. And at the end of it, the elves are very often no further forward than they were at the very beginning.

That is why, when a little elf called Berry saw the notice, he decided at once to ignore it. Berry was a nice little elf, who did his best at everything he tried, but when someone told him not to do something, his elfin nature made him want to rebel.

"I *will* go to the Fair," he said to himself, and he went at once to find a disguise.

As I said before, it is not too difficult to disguise yourself as a fairy if you wear a hat and a cloak, and that is exactly what Berry did, but he had forgotten

that the cloak must be a very
long one, for elfin feet are much,
much larger than fairy ones.

Not realising that his feet were
showing, Berry strolled through
the Fair, until he came to a stall
selling fresh vegetables. Elves
are very fond of vegetables,
especially carrots, so Berry
stopped and looked at what was
on display.

However, it was not long at all
before Berry's attention strayed
from the vegetables and fixed on
the lovely young fairy who was
looking after the stall. She was
the most beautiful little creature
that Berry had ever seen. He

listened as she spoke to her customers and soon realised that she was a very merry, clever little fairy.

A clever little fairy? Berry felt that something was wrong, somewhere. Everyone knew that fairies were silly, didn't they? But the more that Berry listened, the more he realised that fairies are just as lively and intelligent as any elf – and perhaps more so than some.

It wasn't long, either, before Berry realised that the little fairy had noticed him. She spoke kindly to him, which made Berry stammer and blush and fall over himself. The little fairy laughed, and her tinkling voice made Berry's heart turn over. He stayed by the stall all afternoon, occasionally buying vegetables so that he did not look too conspicuous.

By the end of the afternoon, the little fairy found that she liked her young visitor very well, and Berry found that he needed a wheelbarrow to take home all the vegetables he had bought!

Next morning, bright and early, Berry returned to the Fair. He was determined to ask the clever little fairy, whose name, he knew, was Primrose, if he could see her after the Fair had finished, which was the very next day.

Primrose blushed when Berry asked his question.

"I don't know," she said. "I've never had a friend who was an elf before."

"H-h-how did you know?" stammered Berry, blushing to the roots of his hair.

Primrose looked down at Berry's feet and smiled.

"Those aren't fairy feet," she said, shaking her head in fun.

The next day, Berry and Primrose did meet – and the day after that, and the day after *that*. They soon realised that they would like very much to be married, but such a thing had never been heard of before. Primrose decided that the best thing would be to talk to Mother Nature, who understood so many things and might have an answer to this difficult problem.

When the two young people stood before her, Mother Nature smiled. It was so obvious that they were happy together. Berry had taken off his fairy disguise, so it was clear that he was an elf.

"How can I help you, my dears?" asked Mother Nature, although in fact she already knew perfectly well.

"We should like to be married," said Primrose and Berry, "but we are afraid that our families will not be happy. What shall we do?"

"Why, you must talk to them," said wise old Mother Nature. "You, Berry, must show Primrose's family what a fine, upstanding young elf you are, with good prospects and every hope of giving your wife a happy and comfortable life. You should mention that you love her too, of course. And you, Primrose, must show Berry's family that fairies are not the silly creatures they believe them to be. And you should mention that you love him, too."

"We will," said the young couple.

Well, it took a long time to convince both families, but at last they agreed that the young people could be happy. The wedding, which at first was planned to be a small affair, grew and grew, until practically everyone in Elftown and all the local fairies were invited. It was a wonderful party!

Nowadays, fairies and elves all remember that it was at the wedding of Berry and Primrose that they first really saw each other without listening to a lot of silly stories and prejudices. That fairies are clever and elves are kind became clear for all to see.

Nowadays, so many elves and fairies have set up home together that it is no longer wondered at.

Berry and Primrose are very happy together. They have three little children who share all the best features of elves *and* fairies. And each year, the whole family goes to the Fairyland Fair.

The notice outside has changed.

# Fairyland Fair

## Everyone welcome.

### By order of the Fair Committee.

# Oh,
# Florabell!

Everyone knows that fairies are fragile, graceful little creatures. Well, almost all of them are. But there was once a fairy called Florabell who liked cakes. It didn't much matter what kind of cakes they were. Sponge cakes, buns, cherry cakes and chocolate cakes were all favourites. It didn't help that Florabell's mother was an excellent cook, who loved to fill her cake tins with blueberry muffins and caramel slices.

Florabell loved to empty those cake tins as fast as her mother filled them, which was often more than once a day!

I expect you can guess what happens to a fairy who munches cakes all day. Yes, she becomes a well-rounded fairy. Then, if she carries on eating cakes, she becomes a plump fairy. More cakes make her a chubby fairy. Another swiss roll or two and she is a podgy fairy. A couple more visits to the cake tins and there is no doubt about it. That fairy is a fat fairy, and hardly anyone wants to be that.

At the time of this story, Florabell was a chubby, or maybe slightly podgy fairy. She didn't like having to have her dresses let out, but she liked cakes a lot more than she disliked going to the dressmaker. It was no contest really.

At first, Florabell's mother was not at all concerned about her daughter. She liked plump babies and she thought that toddlers really should be cuddly. Florabell seemed to be happy and learning fast. But by the time she was ready to go to school, Florabell was quite a large girl, and her flying was not as good as it should be. That wasn't really surprising. Fairies' wings are delicate little things, meant to lift a fragile fairy from the ground. They were never designed for hoisting hefty girls into orbit.

At last the day came when Florabell's mother took her to the goblin doctor.

"I really can't think why she is *quite* so cuddly," she said.

"I can," said the doctor. "She eats too many sweet things. Why, I saw her munching biscuits in the waiting room."

"She was *hungry*," said Florabell's mother. "A growing girl needs energy."

"Nonsense!" said the doctor. (Goblin doctors are not known for their bedside manners.) "Your daughter needs fresh air, exercise and good food. She does *not* need cakes, or biscuits, or buns. She would not come to any harm if one of those sickly sweet things never passed her lips again. Indeed, she might be a great deal better. And think about her teeth! All those sweet things will do *them* no good at all either. I'm afraid that Florabell must rely on *you* to set a good example as her mother."

Florabell's mother heard this with a sinking heart. She rather enjoyed cakes, and biscuits, and buns too. But she had her daughter's best interests at heart, so when she got home, she put her bakery books well out of reach at the top of the bookshelf and began preparing healthy salads instead.

Over the next few weeks, Florabell's mother got quite a bit thinner. She felt a good deal healthier, too, and would have been able to run energetically about after her little daughter if only that daughter had been running! For Florabell looked exactly the same, or even slightly, well, *chubbier*.

Florabell's mother racked her brains to think of what was going wrong. She was very sure that Florabell was not eating cakes, or biscuits, or buns at home. The teacher at the school assured her that Florabell was not eating naughty things there either.

Florabell's mother was forced to turn detective. For one whole week she kept track of where her little girl went and who she saw. By the end of the week, the poor mother knew where the problem lay – it was Granny.

Florabell's mother went round to see *her* mother straight away. She expected the visit to be difficult, for the old lady enjoyed baking as much as she did.

"Florabell seems to be spending a lot of time with you now," the little girl's mother began.

"Oh yes," said Granny. "It's lovely. She always calls in after school. Poor wee mite, she's so hungry after a busy afternoon that she can't make that long journey home unless she has a little snack here. I often give her something to put in her lunchbox for the next day as well. I don't want to criticise, dear, but a child can't live on tomatoes alone. She's not very fond of salad."

Florabell's mother restrained herself with difficulty. All these weeks of lettuce, and it seemed that the only person who had been eating it was herself!

"You're looking a little peaky, dear," said her mother. "I don't think you're eating properly. Let me get you a nice slice of cake and some hot chocolate. Florabell loves that."

"No, thank you, Mother," said Florabell's mummy, and she proceeded to explain to the old lady exactly why it was important not to give Florabell the sweet things she obviously loved so much.

It took quite a lot of explaining before Granny got the message. She loved her granddaughter so much that she found it difficult to think of her as anything but completely perfect.

Florabell's mummy had to smile when she looked at her own mother. The old lady loved cakes as much as anyone, but she was much slimmer and more active even than her daughter.

"I know *you* seem to be able to eat anything and never put on an ounce of weight," said Florabell's mother, "but the rest of us aren't like that. We have to be much more careful about what we eat."

"Well, I try to keep active," said her mother with a smile. "Our little Florabell should do more running about."

"When?" asked her daughter. "The children laugh at her during sports lessons at school."

"Well, after school then," said Florabell's granny.

"After school she's *here*," said Florabell's mummy, "filling her little tummy with sweet things."

"You're right," said the old lady at last. "I've been trying to be kind to my little darling, but instead I've been causing her harm. You just leave it to me. I'll put things right, I promise."

Over the next few weeks, Florabell continued to go to Granny's house after school, but she didn't get any plumper. In fact, she began to look a little bit thinner, and she had a pinkness in her cheeks and a brightness in her eyes that had never been there before.

"You don't have to go to Granny's house *every* night," said her mother gently one evening, as she tucked her little daughter into bed.

"Oh yes, I do," said Florabell, "poor Granny needs me."

"Does she?" asked her mother, thinking of the lively and happy old lady she knew and loved. "Why is that exactly, darling?"

"Well, she has a terrible urge to eat sweet, sticky things that are bad for her teeth and, at her age, almost every part of her," said Florabell seriously. "She needs me to be there to stop her doing it. I've had to be careful not to eat things like that in front of her, so that I don't upset her."

"Have you?" asked her mother with a smile. "That's very kind of you. But don't you miss those things yourself?"

"Not if it's for Granny's sake," said the little girl firmly. "I'd do anything in the world for her."

There was no doubt about it, Florabell was soon beginning to look not so much chubby as plump. And pretty soon after that, she began to seem not so much plump as well-rounded.

Florabell seemed to have so much more energy now, too. One day, her mother found her practising skipping in the garden.

"That's very good, darling," she said. "I didn't know you could skip so well."

"Oh," said Florabell, "I have to, for Granny, you know."

"Really?" asked her mother.

"Oh, yes. The doctor has told Granny that she must skip for

half an hour a day. She finds it
*so* hard to do, poor old thing. I
have to practise really hard so
that I can show her how. Then I
do her exercises with her to
make sure she does them
properly. You know, if I'm not
there every minute, she just
stops. Isn't that silly? Everyone
knows it's important to do
exercise, don't they."

"Yes," said Mummy with a
smile. "You're quite right."

"Which reminds me," said her
slim little girl. "you need to skip
too. You never do any exercise."

"Oh, Florabell!" laughed her
mummy. "Oh, Mother!"

# The Forest
# Fairy

When you ask someone what they know about fairies, they often talk about the way that they are small and pretty. They will probably mention the fact that they have gauzy little wings and can fly. And last of all, they will mention the fact that they have fairy wands. You know the kind of thing – a little stick with a star on top.

Now the fact is that most fairies don't have wands at all. When they are flying about in the countryside, they really need both hands free to help other living things. Most of the time, a wand would get in the way.

So where have we got this wand idea from? Well, not many people have seen fairies, as you know. You may have been one of the lucky ones. A long time ago, someone saw a little fairy carrying a fallen star back to its place in the sky. Young stars sometimes do slip. They need to be put gently back in place, using a special star stick.

I can see that you need me to
explain about star sticks, too.
The fact is, although stars can
look cold and glittery in the sky,
in fact they are rather hot. In
order not to burn their little
fingers, fairies pick them up on
the end of a stick, called a star
stick. That way, they can pop
them back into the sky without
any problem.

You can imagine what
happened. The human being long
ago caught sight of a fairy just as
she was flying up to put the star
back. He didn't know about star
sticks, so he assumed that what
she was carrying was a magic

wand. He was so excited about what he saw that he told lots and lots of other people. And that is how the story about fairy wands was spread.

Now it is a funny thing about rumours. Sometimes they spread so far and so fast that they almost become true, especially if they get back to the person they are about.

After the silly human had seen what he thought was a fairy wand, one of the people he told was a friend of his, who was a painter. Before you could say "Stardust nonsense," the painter had made a portrait of the fairy his friend had described, and, of course, she was carrying a fairy wand. This picture became quite famous, but still, it would not have been seen by very many people, if some bright spark had not decided to print a small version of it on to the postage stamps of a large country. They looked so pretty that other countries copied the idea, and soon there was hardly anyone in the whole world who had not seen the picture of the fairy with her star stick – or fairy wand as they thought.

In case you are interested, this is what the picture looked like:

Now I'm sure you will agree with me that the picture does not look like any of the fairies we have seen. But most of the people who saw the stamp had no idea what a fairy should look like. They thought it was a lovely picture and left it at that.

But the trouble is that human beings always leave an incredible amount of rubbish lying about. Fairies are constantly clearing up what people leave behind, and some of the things they throw away so carelessly are used envelopes. That is how several fairies saw the famous stamps and the picture of the fairy carrying a star stick and a fallen star.

Now you may remember me telling you that each kind of fairy has a special job to do. Moonflower Fairies keep the moon bright and polished, so that it shines down on us each night. If they didn't, that old moon would get terribly dusty, sitting up in the sky. Sunflower Fairies make sure that the faces of even the shyest little flowers are turned towards the sun each morning. Of course, it is Starflower Fairies that put the stars back in the sky when they have fallen to earth by mistake.

A fairy who works in deserts or woodlands or rivers may never have met a Starflower Fairy, just as they are not likely to have met a Tigerlily Fairy (who has a very dangerous job concerning tigers, which I will not go into here). So when these other fairies saw the human postage stamp with the picture of a fairy on it, even they thought she might be carrying a magic wand. That is the way that silly stories are spread.

"I wish I could have a magic wand," said one little fairy to her mother one day. "It would look just right with my new dress."

"Well, I haven't got one, Briar Rose," her mother said, "and I don't know any other fairy who has. I think they must be some kind of special thing that only fairies in pictures have. I've met a lot of fairies in my time, and not one of them has had a fairy wand."

Briar Rose always believed what her mother said, of course, but she believed the evidence of her own eyes, too. She knew what she had seen on the postage stamp, and she still thought that the fairy wand looked very pretty. If there were wands to be had, she wanted one. And she wanted it badly.

Week after week, Briar Rose saved up her pocket money. She did not know how much a fairy wand would cost, but she made a sensible guess. When she thought she had enough, she went along to the general store in Goblinville.

Now goblins, as well as being very good doctors, are also excellent shopkeepers. They are sensible about money and clever enough to keep a track of what they have in stock so that they never (well, hardly ever) run out.

The goblin who kept the general store in Goblinville smiled at Briar Rose when she came into the shop with a serious expression on her pretty face. It showed she meant business.

"What can I do for you, young lady?" he asked.

"Please," said Briar Rose, holding out her pocket money, "I'd like to buy a fairy wand."

"A fairy wand?" said the goblin. "I'm afraid we don't have any call for those. You are the first fairy ever to ask me for one. I'm quite sure that I don't have one in stock at the moment, but if you would be kind enough to wait just a moment, I will get my big catalogue and see if I could send away for one for you. It would only take a day or two."

So the goblin went into the back of his shop and came back with a huge, dusty book. It was so large that he was staggering as he carried it back to his counter and set it down.

"Now, let's have a look," he muttered, leafing through the pages. "*D* for dragons, *E* for elves, aha! Here's *F* for fairies."

The little fairy held her breath. She looked down at the money clutched in her little hand and wondered how expensive a fairy wand would be.

*"Fairy dresses, fairy furniture fairy hats, fairy pots and pans, fairy stockings, fairy wings …*

hmm, nothing here about fairy wands, I'm afraid."

But Briar Rose's attention had been caught by another item in the catalogue.

"*Fairy wings?*" she asked. "You can't buy fairy wings, can you?"

"No, no," laughed the goblin, "when I saw that it wasn't about wands, I stopped reading. That entry is for *fairy wings, special non-drying soap for.*"

"*Special non-drying soap for* doesn't make sense," said Briar Rose with a puzzled look.

"I'm sorry," smiled the goblin, looking down kindly at the little fairy. "I'm not explaining very well. The catalogue puts the most important part of the item first, even if it isn't the first part. The entry should read: *Special non-drying soap for fairy wings.*"

"Do I need that?" asked Briar Rose, trying to look over her shoulder at her own little wings.

"No, no," said the goblin. "I only sell that to older fairies, whose wings have become a little wrinkly, you know. Your own wings are quite beautiful as they are. Now, about this fairy wand…"

Briar Rose remembered why she had come to the shop, and that there had been no mention of a fairy wand in the catalogue.

"Could it be under something else?" she asked, now that she understood how the catalogue worked. "Like *wand, fairy* or *wand, magic*."

"I see you're getting the idea," smiled the goblin. "Let's have a look, shall we?"

But although they looked at lots of different entries, there was no mention of fairy wands in the catalogue at all.

"As I said," the goblin advised, "it's not something I've ever been asked for before. Are you sure there are such things?"

Then Briar Rose explained about the postage stamp she had

seen on a human letter. She described it in every detail.

"Well," said the goblin. "I'm not sure I would rely on anything that a human being paints. They're not very clever. I happen to know that they have the most extraordinarily silly ideas about goblins. If the fairy wand is as simple as you say, why don't you make your own?"

"Could I?" asked Briar Rose.

"Well, I think so," said the goblin. "It doesn't sound very difficult to me. I can give you a stick and some glue. All you have to do is to find a star. I'm afraid we don't sell those either."

He really was a very kind goblin. When Briar Rose stretched out her little hand to give him her pocket money, he shook his head.

"No, no," he said. "The stick and the glue are free. You might need your pocket money on your star-finding adventures. Good luck, little fairy!"

Clutching her stick and the glue, the little fairy hurried off to tell her mother what had happened. But her mother was out stroking pine needles with her gentle fingers, so that they all lay in one direction, not standing up on end like a hedgehog!

Briar Rose left the stick and the
glue in a safe place and set off to
find a star. The only thing she
really knew about stars was that
they were found in the sky. (She'd
never heard, you see, of falling
stars or the fairies who rescue
them.) With her little nose in the
air, Briar Rose set off in search of
a shining star.

You and I, being wiser and
older than Briar Rose, will know
that she was not very likely to
find a star in the daytime. You
need a dark, clear night to see
stars at their best. But Briar Rose
didn't know that. She searched
the skies until it was almost dark,

but she could not find a single shining star.

Then, just as the sun was going down, and the sky was taking on a lovely deep blue colour, the little fairy saw something shining in the distance. She hurried towards it, quite forgetting to notice where she was.

At last she came to the very edge of the forest. One tree stood by itself, a little way from the others. As the little fairy watched, she was astonished and delighted to see something twinkling on top of the tree. She moved closer, hardly daring to breathe. It was! It was! At the top of the tree was a little shining star, perfect for a fairy wand!

Briar Rose was so excited, she didn't think about anything else. Although it was getting dark now, she was determined not to go home until she had got her star.

Using all her strength, the little fairy flew up, up, up into the air. It was farther than she had ever flown before, but at last, just when she felt that her little wings wouldn't flutter any more, she reached the top of the tree.

But the star wasn't there. The little fairy looked up. There was the star, shining so far above her that the little fairy gave a sigh of disappointment. It had only looked as if the star was sitting on top of the tree. Now she realised that it was high above it, right up in the clear night sky. Briar Rose knew that she would never, never be able to fly so far.

Feeling sad and disappointed, the little fairy flew down to the ground. It was time to go home.

But oh dear, it was properly dark now, and each tree looked the same as its neighbour. For the first time, Briar Rose felt a little worried. No one knew where she was. They could not come to rescue her. What if she had to stay here, in the cold and dark, until morning? The thought made the little fairy shiver and shake.

As she sat under the single tree, Briar Rose heard the little squeaks and cries of the forest night. Her mother had explained to her that these were nothing to be frightened of, but it was different, somehow, when they were so near and she was on her own. Now, more than anything, Briar Rose wished her mummy, with her warm, comforting arms, was nearby.

Just then, a voice floated through the trees.

"Briar Rose! Briar Rose! Where are you?"

It *was* her mummy! In no time at all, the little fairy was safe.

"How did you find me?" she asked her relieved mother.

Then Mummy explained that she had gone to the goblin shop and heard all about the fairy wand.

"When we get home," she said, "I will make you a star from silver paper to put on the end of your wand. It will only be pretend, but I'm afraid that the picture on the stamp is only pretend too."

"That will be lovely," said Briar Rose. "My wand will be magic because *you* made it. It doesn't need a real star."

And, you know, she was right!

# The
# Furious
# Fairy

Now some of the stories that are told in books are true, and some of them are not. This one was told to me by a very old lady, who claimed to have had many fairy friends when she was young. You will have to make up your own mind about whether you believe it or not.

Once upon a time, there were twelve good fairies who lived in a certain kingdom. One day, they were invited to the baptism of the baby daughter of the King and Queen of the kingdom. They were happy to go and give the little Princess all the blessings within their power.

Unfortunately, the King and Queen had completely forgotten to invite the thirteenth fairy, who was very old and lived in a cave in the mountains.

They had not heard from her for several years, so they thought she might have moved away.

But the thirteenth fairy heard about the Princess's birth and the party that was to be held to celebrate her baptism. And she was absolutely *furious*!

Now, you are probably thinking that this story sounds rather familiar. Doesn't the thirteenth fairy come and curse the little Princess, so that she pricks her finger on a spindle and falls asleep for a hundred years?

Well, I have read the story you are thinking of in many books, and that is exactly what happens, but it is not the story I want to tell you here. This story is not about the Princess at all. It is about what happened to the thirteenth fairy when she went back to her mountain home.

Have you ever done anything naughty? Really naughty? No? Are you sure? Well, if you have ever done something just a little bit naughty, you will know that you can have a rather funny feeling afterwards.

It's a feeling that makes you think maybe there's something squiggling in your tummy. And there's a funny feeling in your head as well. It's as though the only thing you can think about is that silly, naughty thing you did. I'm afraid there is only one cure for a feeling like that. You have to go and say sorry for the naughty thing, and if possible, you must put right everything that has gone wrong. Then, if the people involved are kind to you and understand that you will never, ever do the naughty thing again, they will smile and say you are forgiven, and you will feel much, much better, with no more squiggly feelings.

Now, you can imagine, that if you have squiggly feelings after you have done a very little naughty thing, you must have really bad wriggly, jiggly, squiggly feelings after you have done a very bad thing. That is what happened to the thirteenth fairy, as you will hear.

After she had cursed the baby Princess and crashed the palace doors shut behind her, the thirteenth fairy flew away from the castle as fast as her wings would carry her. Normally, the guards in the palace would have stopped anyone who came to do harm to the King and Queen and their little one. But the guests and servants in the palace were all so shocked by what had happened that they could not move for several minutes. Then they were busy making sure that they baby was all right. It was only about five minutes later that guards came rushing out to find the

thirteenth fairy, and by then she was far, far away, flying over the mountains towards her cave.

But, if the truth be told, the furious fairy was not flying very well. Those jiggly, wriggly, squiggly feelings had been joined by a wiggly feeling in her tummy. It is hard to fly with all that going on inside you, as you can imagine. And perhaps that is why the furious fairy didn't make it back to her cave. She took her attention away from what she was doing for just a second too long and crash-landed in the middle of a wood. *Woosh! Wallop! Woomph!* And she was down.

Fairies are usually excellent flyers. Their safety record is second to none, as they are sensible enough not to fly into windows, as birds sometimes do, or try to do difficult low-flying manoeuvres when it is foggy. For this reason, fairies are not trained what to do in the event of an aerial accident. The furious fairy lay in the bush where she had fallen with no idea what to do next. She did not think that she was badly hurt, but she could not be sure.

It was then that she saw the bear! It was a big, brown, furry bear, and it was heading straight towards her, making a little growling noise as it came.

Now most bears are much more frightened of humans than humans are of them. But fairies are different. Bears *like* fairies, as they rely on them to tell them when to wake up after their long winter's sleep. In the old days, when bears decided for themselves when to go outside in search of food, they made some dreadful mistakes. One warm day was enough to wake them, but it might be in the middle of winter! A bear often wandered away from his cave in search of food only to find that the next day the snow was falling thick and fast so that he couldn't find his way home again. Since fairies took over the job, things have been much better. You hardly ever see a bear until the snow has started to melt and spring is well and truly on the way.

However, the furious fairy had no experience of bears. All she felt when she saw one coming towards her was that the squiggly, wriggly feeling had come back with a vengeance. She tried to sit up so that she could escape, but somehow she felt very wobbly, which is not surprising after a fall.

The bear came closer and closer to the furious fairy, until she could feel his hot breath on her face.

"Hmmm," said the bear. "What have we here?"

The furious fairy was so astonished to hear the bear talking her language that she forgot to be frightened for a moment. In fact, the bear was talking Bear, but fairies are very good at understanding all kinds of languages. The furious fairy had been such a bad-tempered unpleasant old fairy for so long that she had not even tried to communicate with other living things. She had completely forgotten that her old fairy skills were just rusty.

The furious fairy felt that it would be a good idea to reply to the bear.

"I've had an accident," she said, in an every softer voice than fairies usually use.

Luckily, bears always have excellent hearing.

"I can see that," said the bear. "Can I help at all?"

"I don't think so," said the thirteenth fairy, amazed that another creature should be so kind to her. "I don't think I've broken anything. It's just that the fall took my breath away, and it hasn't all come back yet."

Without another word, the bear picked her up in his strong, furry arms and turned towards a winding forest path.

"Hey! Just a minute!" called the fairy. "Where are you taking me?"

"I'm taking you back to my cave," said the bear. "You're very thin and you've had a big shock. I'll look after you until you feel well enough to fly home."

The furious fairy was about to protest, but really, she didn't feel too energetic at the moment, and the idea of something to eat was very appealing. She realised that she had not had a proper meal since she heard about the baby Princess's baptism and realised that she had not been invited. The news had made a hard, cold lump in her tummy that made it difficult to eat.

They soon arrived at the bear's cave. The fairy looked round with pleasure. She was used to caves, for she lived in one herself, and this one was very fine. The bear had a lovely soft bed and a little ledge where he ate his food. It was very cosy.

And a snack of fruit and nuts was most welcome too. The fairy ate ravenously.

When she had finished, she felt warm and full, so when the bear asked her why she had not eaten recently, she told him all about the non-existent invitation to the Princess's baptism and how it had made her feel cold and unwanted and cross.

"So what did you do about it?" asked the bear. "Did you get in touch with the palace and point out that they had made a mistake, so that they could put it right?"

"No," said the fairy.

"Did you send a present anyway, to show that there were no hard feelings?"

"No," said the fairy.

"So you just felt upset for a while but did nothing?"

"No," said the fairy. She could feel the squiggly, wriggly, jiggly feelings in her tummy again, and they were worse than ever.

Very slowly, not looking at him, the fairy told the bear what she had done.

When she looked up, the bear was shaking his big brown head.

"Oh dear," he said. "Oh dear. Oh dear. Oh dear. That's bad. That's very bad."

"I know," said the fairy. "But what's done is done. I shouldn't have got so cross, perhaps, but those other fairies were all being so goody-goody. It made me mad down to my boots."

"So what are you going to do now?" asked the bear.

"Do? Well, I'm going to go home to my cave and carry on as usual," said the fairy, but even as she said it, she knew that she would have to do more than that.

"I don't think that will take away your squiggly, wiggly feeling," said the bear seriously.

"How do you know about *that*?" cried the fairy in surprise.

"Don't you know what that feeling is?" asked the bear. "It's your conscience. It's telling you that you must put what you did right, or you will never feel really happy again."

"Is it?" asked the fairy. She dimly remembered her old mother saying something similar, many, many years ago. How very strange. She knew in her heart of hearts that the bear was right.

It was a few days before the furious fairy was ready to travel.

"Come back and see me when everything is sorted out!" called the bear, as he waved goodbye to the thirteenth fairy.

Very sensibly, the fairy put on a disguise to return to the palace. She found that everyone was still talking about what had happened at the baptism, and she heard too of the way in which the twelfth fairy had softened her curse.

"Thank goodness," said the thirteenth fairy. "That is just what I would have done myself. Now I must wait until I can break the spell for ever."

Years passed. The thirteenth fairy went about her business as usual, but now she took a special interest in the woodland creatures who lived around her cave. She was a much nicer fairy now.

At last the fairy had news from a passing bird that the whole royal palace had fallen into a deep sleep.

"No harm can come to them while they are sleeping," she said, and settled down to wait again.

Ninety-nine years later, the fairy was off on her travels again. She flew to a distant country, where a fine young prince was living. One night, the fairy crept into his room and whispered in his ear. In the morning, the Prince suddenly announced that he wanted to go travelling. The rest of the story, I think you know.

And the furious fairy? She and her friend the bear attend every royal function, including a recent wedding that I hear was very special indeed.

# Fairies to
# the
# Rescue!

What do you do if a kitten gets stuck in a tree? Well, you stand at the bottom and call him. You hold up his bowl of kitty food and try to tempt him down. You try being cross and you try being nice. You may even point out the nice strong branch that he should jump on to. But the chances are that none of these ideas will work. Kittens, once they get stuck, seem to get well and truly stuck. And somehow, they can't remember exactly how they managed to climb up to where they are now. If only they could remember where they had put each little paw. Coming down would be so much easier. But kittens are not as sensible as fairies. They prefer just to sit in the tree and wait to be rescued.

When all other ideas have been tried, most people call the fire brigade. These fine people are usually only too happy to help, as long as they are not busy fighting a fire, of course.

Along comes the fire engine. When it gets very near, it flashes its lights to amuse the children. Then the engine parks safely by the side of the road, and the firefighters get out.

"Where's the little rascal?" they ask, peering up into the tree.

And there he is, sitting on his branch, looking pathetically down at the ground.

"No problem" say the brave firefighters. "We'll have him down in no time."

Up go the long, long ladders, and up go the firefighters. Nearer and nearer to the little kitten they come until ... have they got him? Yes ... no ... yes ...oh! *Just* before the first firefighter reaches the kitten, he jumps down from his branch and runs merrily down the tree into your arms!

Ask any firefighter and he or she will tell you that happens all the time.

Now most people believe that the reason for the kitten's annoying behaviour is that it just doesn't want to be caught. When the firefighter comes near, its fear vanishes and it skips down the tree to avoid those reaching hands.

But what really happens is very different. Shall I let you into a secret? Don't tell, will you?

It is fairies who are to blame! Yes, fairies, who are normally such good and kind little creatures, just occasionally like to have a joke.

They flutter up into the tree with the kitten and say, "Stay where you are until we say the word. This is a good game, isn't it?" And the kitten is only too happy to play along.

So next time you see a kitten apparently trapped in a tree, look very carefully at the leaves and branches nearby. You just might see a cheeky little face peeping out at you, if you look hard enough!

# The Dew Drop Fairy

Have you ever been out in the early morning, before the sun has had a chance to dry the grass? You will find that every little blade of green has a sparkling dew drop on its tip. It looks so pretty if the sunlight makes the dew drops twinkle, and it's the Dew Drop Fairy that we have to thank for it.

The Dew Drop Fairy is always up and about before the sun has risen, and she has gone back to the shelter of her little toadstool home by the time the sun is high in the sky. She has spent so long among dew drops that she fears she would melt away as they do if

she had to sit in the hot sun.

One day, the Dew Drop Fairy received a letter written on a leaf. That is how fairies usually send their messages, and they give them to little birds who are flying in the right direction for delivery.

This leaf had come a very, very long way. It was from the Dew Drop Fairy's cousin in the rainforests of South America.

I don't know if you have ever read about the rainforest. It is a wonderful place, where thousands and thousands of plants and animals make their homes. In fact, there are probably hundreds of kinds of insect that human beings have never seen, although fairies, of course, know them well.

The Dew Drop Fairy's cousin was called the Pitcher Plant Fairy. She had a special job to do. In the rainforest there are curious plants that live high up in the trees. Their roots do not reach down to the ground but are lodged in the bark of the trees on whose branches they perch. They take some of the food they need from the trees, and the trees don't seem to mind.

Now the curious thing about these plants is that they have a little basin in the middle. Where the petals meet at the centre, there is a hollow part, which fills up with water. It is the Pitcher Plant Fairy's job to make sure that the pitcher plant is always full of water. You are probably wondering why this matters, but the fact is that lots of little insects and animals rely on their treetop basin for water. Some little frogs even sit in the pitcher plant's pool all day, high up in the trees! They never come down to splash in an ordinary pool.

The Pitcher Plant Fairy told her cousin about the wonderful rainforest in her letter, and she finished up with even more exciting news.

"The rains are coming," she said, "so my work is not needed for a while. I am coming to visit you by the next available seabird."

The Dew Drop Fairy was terribly excited. She hurried about, making sure that her house was neat and tidy and her spare bed was made up with thistledown pillows and a blanket of sheep's wool, gleaned from the hedges and fences where the sheep leave it.

The Dew Drop Fairy wasn't sure when exactly her cousin was coming, but she kept a sharp look out whenever any large birds flew overhead. At last, one sunny morning, she heard a squawk outside and rushed out to find her cousin saying goodbye to a black-headed gull.

"Thank you so much for bringing me," said the fairy.

"Don't mention it," replied the bird. "I was glad of the company."

Well, the Dew Drop Fairy was glad of the company too. She

hurried her cousin into the house and begged her to sit down to rest after her long journey.

"Oh, we never rest in the rainforest," said her cousin, who was wearing a bright red and green and blue costume. "We are on the go all the time," she went on. "There's something about the steamy heat of the forest that is very invigorating."

"Oh, I shouldn't like that at all," said the Dew Drop Fairy. "I don't like to go out in the sunshine, for fear that I would melt away like my own dew drops."

"That's nonsense, surely," said her cousin briskly. "Fairies don't melt away. They're much too well made for that."

The Pitcher Plant Fairy looked critically at her cousin.

"You look so pale," she said, "almost like a ghost, but it's not surprising if you never go out into the sunshine. If there's one thing I'll do while I'm here, it's to introduce you to a little light and warmth. Just look at your grey-green clothes. How dull they are."

"I couldn't wear bright colours like yours in my job," said the Dew Drop Fairy. "Why, human beings out for an early morning walk with their dogs would spot me easily on the green grass. And that would be the end of me, I can assure you."

"Really?" asked the Pitcher Plant Fairy. "Are humans in your world so dangerous? In the rainforest, the Indians love to catch sight of us among the leaves. They would never dream of doing us harm. My clothes are bright to fit in with the other rainforest creatures. You should see the parrots with their brilliant feathers! They are much more beautiful than anything you have here. Look, I've brought some little pictures for you to see."

The Dew Drop Fairy looked curiously at the pictures of

parrots and colourful frogs. There were flowers too, in bright, hot colours. They made the flowers that the Dew Drop Fairy was used to look rather dull and drab.

At first, the Dew Drop Fairy was happy to hear stories of the amazing place where her cousin lived, but before long she began to be tired of it. It all sounded so bright and vivid, she felt that her own tender senses would never stand it.

"Come back with me," begged her cousin. "It's only fair. I've seen where you live. Now you must come and visit me. I can tell just by looking at you that you

don't get out much. A change will
do you all the good in the world.

"Let me think about it," said the
Dew Drop Fairy.

Next morning,while her visitor
was still in bed, the Dew Drop
Fairy went out to sprinkle dew
drops as usual. She soon finished
her work and stopped to look
over the gentle countryside.

"It's lovely, isn't it?" said Mother Nature, coming up behind her. "Of course, I love all the living things in the world, but this lovely scene, with its gentle colours, is one of my favourites. And I love the sharp scent of autumn in the air. You know, in some places, they have no seasons. It is the same all year round. I prefer our changing scene."

"So do I," said the fairy.

So the Dew Drop Fairy didn't go to South America, although she does now sometimes venture into the sunshine. "I live in the loveliest place on earth," she says. "Just as my cousin does!"

# The
# Cobweb
# Collector

Once upon a time, there was a little fairy who loved to collect cobwebs. It wasn't part of her usual job, but she found them so useful, she could never have enough of them. From the lacy cobwebs, the little fairy made all kinds of beautiful things. She knitted them into shawls and wove them into hammocks. She used the threads to tie up little parcels and to moor her oak-leaf boat to the bank. She really did not know what she would do without cobwebs. Eventually, although it was not her real name, everyone called her the Cobweb Fairy.

Now there was only one creature who loved cobwebs more than the little fairy I have described, and that was the spider who spun them! He liked to spin several webs in different places. Then he would go round and visit them in turn to see if he had caught any flies. You can imagine his annoyance when he found on a regular basis that several of his favourite cobwebs were missing!

The spider understood that cobwebs are fragile things, and accidents will happen. He knew that sometimes the wind would blow them away, and occasionally a bird will fly into one or a passing human thoughtlessly brush it down. But all those events leave little threads behind to wave in the air. Someone, the spider realised, was snipping his cobwebs neatly through and collecting them on purpose.

There was only one thing to do. The spider lay in wait by one of his webs. As soon as the Cobweb Fairy arrived with her little scissors, he darted out and wrapped her tightly in one of his sticky threads.

"What do you mean by stealing my precious cobwebs?" he asked.

"I'm sorry," said the fairy.

"Do you usually steal things?" asked the spider.

"No, no. I didn't think I was stealing. I thought the webs were abandoned. You weren't here, after all. How was I to know?"

The spider could tell that she was telling the truth. And she had a fair point. He didn't in the least mind if she took his old webs.

"We'll have to think of a sort of signal," he said.

So now, when the spider is ready to abandon a web, he weaves a special pattern in it to tell the Cobweb Fairy. Look very carefully at cobwebs – but don't touch them – and you may see it, too!

# Your Own
# Special
# Fairy

Did you know that you have your own special fairy? It's true. There is a little fairy whose job it is just to look after you. She tries hard to keep you safe and to make sure that you are happy, but sometimes that is not an easy job. Children often make it difficult for their own special fairies to do their best.

For one thing, it is very important that you believe in your fairy. No fairy can work well if she thinks that people are not taking her seriously. The best way to let your fairy know that you appreciate everything she is doing for you is to think about her from time to time. Your fairy can read your thoughts (although other fairies cannot), and she will glow with pride to know that you are wishing her well.

If you shut your eyes now, and sit very still, and think about your fairy and how you imagine she looks, you may just feel her settling ever so gently on your shoulder. If you open your eyes, she will fly away so quickly that you will only just see a fluttering and a movement out of the corner of your eye.

So what does your fairy look like? I can tell you, even though I don't know what *you* look like!

She has hair of ... your colour! She has eyes of ... your colour! Her skin is like yours and so is her smile. Can you see her a little more clearly now?

When you are ill, your fairy is very sad, but she never leaves your side. Even in the middle of the night, she sits by your head, stroking your hair so gently that you cannot even feel it.

When you are naughty, your fairy is sad too. She begins to feel faint and ill, wondering if you will be good again to make her feel better. For fairies do not like other people to be unhappy, and sooner or later you being naughty

will make someone else's life a little bit worse than it was before.

When you are good, your fairy almost shimmers with pride. She likes to boast about you to other fairies, saying, "My child is so kind and thoughtful. You could not find a prouder fairy than me."

And when you are ready for bed, your fairy sings a little song, especially for you.

*Here I am, your fairy friend,*
*I'll be with you to night's end.*
*If you're good I'll be so glad,*
*But I'm sorry when you're bad.*

*Fairies one and fairies all,*
*Fairies short and fairies tall,*
*Fairies gather in a ring,*
*Hear the song that fairies sing.*

*If you treat me as you should,*
*Being kind and being good,*
*I will love you dearly too,*
*Always looking after you.*

*Fairies one and fairies all,*
*Fairies short and fairies tall,*
*Fairies gather in a ring,*
*Hear the song that fairies sing.*

*When you're ill or not too well,*
*Listen for my tinkling bell.*
*When you hear it, you will see*
*That you can rely on me.*

*Fairies one and fairies all,*
*Fairies short and fairies tall,*
*Fairies gather in a ring,*
*Hear the song that fairies sing.*